THAT KID

Kurt J

PublishAmerica
Baltimore

Softcover 9781629077833
PUBLISHED BY PUBLISHAMERICA, LLLP
www.publishamerica.com
Baltimore

Printed in the United States of America

(Metropolitan)- buildings-buses-cars-cabs and people- It's summertime- Minneapolis, Minnesota – summer of 1963-

Pearl and Shirley are two young beautiful black women sitting on the sofa having dinner and watching TV- Pearl is expecting a child, she is sitting down- Big brother James is playing with little sister Susie (in the back ground)- The TV is viewing, comedy-The Honey Mooners"- all of a sudden! / Pearl is in severe pain! Pearl is rushed to the hospital immediately!

Now Marlow (The dad) is *who knows where- somewhere outside shooting dice with his hoodlum friends- talking smack, guys pushing each other around- playing music-
Al Green- Love and happiness– old Cadillac's parked about-

Pearl is on a hospital bed being rushed to the emergency room- (everybody is frantic!) little James and Susie are being escorted to the waiting room- Shirley is by Pearl's side, she asks the Doctor hysterically: "is my sister going to be alright?"
The doctor does not reply, (he is to intensely into saving Pearl)-

Pearl is at the end of her labor, and has a baby boy, (she seems to recover very well from her labor,) but is immensely tired- the only problem is- she finds: that the baby has no heart beat!

Pearl is truly sad; she almost dies from having the child; and all the trouble she went through- for what? For carrying this child for practically nine months! (The doctor and Shirley are still in the room)- Pearl decides, she is going to pray- the doctor he decides to try one more procedure- as Pearl is praying- the sunlight begins to fall upon the hospital room (as though it's light became of amber) - (you're the best thing that ever happened to me) - about the same time- the doctor injects the small infant in the heart with a tiny little needle- *Lo and behold- it is a miracle! The child, he lives! Pearl, the Doctor and Shirley are so full of silent joy! That's when Pearl says: "I think I will name him Elliott- yes I will name my son- Elliott, Elliott Jay"

Elliott was a little older now and mom and dad were not living together (they didn't really see much of each other) - Marlow was always away- (always on the run, hustling) - Marlow is in a bar playing cards and catches a guy (who thinks he can pull a fast one over on him by cheating!) ("What a Back Stabber") Marlow tells his boys to take him out back and Marlow beats the crap out of him for cheating, and then takes his money! Elliott, he too was always up to no good (even as a small child)- Although* It seemed at times Elliott had had bad luck- One time Elliott had a bee fly right into his ear! His best friend was very smart and suggested to Elliott- just how to get that bee out, by placing his hand against his ear causing pressure- it worked!

Elliott loved riding in cars (he rode in them all the time- once, he shoved a bobby pin in an electric socket- (pretending it was the ignition to a car) "BOY WHAT A SHOCK THAT WAS!" Of course he was all right! And Elliott, he loved horses too- he'd draw them on his bedroom wall with coloring crayons- he was pretty good at drawing them too! That's just how much Elliott enjoyed them! One night, Elliott placed his rocking horse on his bed- *and he fell right off of his horse- smacked down (face first) right to the floor! He didn't get hurt (not too badly-just his pride)-

Another night, Marlow came over to the house and took Elliott on his motorcycle- Marlow was always showing off with all of his cars and motorcycles- He would actually perform crazy stunts- like riding wheelies on his motorbike while giving a ride to pregnant Aunt Shirley! Imagine that- So Marlow would set Elliott right on the front bars of his motorbike (because Elliott was too small to sit anywhere else)- The two would cruise down by the railroad tracks- Marlow would bring Elliott back to the house safe and sound- Marlow would tuck Elliott in Elliott's tiny old bed- and this time Marlow placed a large ring on Elliott's tiny little finger- you see, Marlow always gave things that were way too big for Elliott- but he loved his little boy anyway- Marlow wanted Elliott to end up better than he did-

One day Marlow took Elliott to one of his "Red Light Party's" (to show off his little boy- "He could never say goodbye"- Marlow has a conversation with one of his thuggish buddies: "I'll bet you One Hundred dollars that my little boy here can actually take this small time piece *here apart and put it back together again, and within ten minutes"! Marlow's homey laugh and said: "Marlow, you're crazier than I thought you were- but you've got you a bet- (Sucker)!" As sure as the night was long- Little Elliott completed his task- and exceptionally well! The people were amazed!

The very next day, Elliott goes down the street to see his best friend Tina- they would play innocently and Elliott just loved being over at Tina's house, especially playing with the toy guitar and little organ that Tina had in her room (they would play for hours) - (Elliott went home) - Pearl, was worried about little Elliott and say's to him: "BOY, I DO NOT WANT

YOU TO GO DOWN TO THAT LITTLE GIRL'S HOUSE NO MORE, YOU HEAR ME!" She screamed! Did Elliott listen? (Probably not) he would never listen to his mother, he was always hard headed.

Elliott just loved guitars- The way they sounded, (not to mention) the different colors, shapes and sizes- He loved them so much; that he would pretend that he was actually playing on one in the Christmas catalog! Elliott would hope that one day he could receive a guitar for Christmas- a guitar of his very own- Elliott would bounce on the couch (bobbing his head back and forth) and all he would ever listen to was: "The Jackson Five" until he would wear a groove print (with his head) in the couch-

The next day- Elliott and his sister Susie went to the store for some groceries (about six or eight blocks away) Elliott and Susie would sometimes argue- Elliott had a bag of groceries and so did Susie- Elliott asked his older sister Susie to hold the bag while he would tie his tennis shoe- of course they were arguing first-

As soon as Elliott had tied his tennis shoe up- like the speed of light!

Elliott took off running faster than a cat falling from an old tree! As soon as Susie got home, she was looking for Elliott! She was on the hunt! "Where's Elliott? Where is he- I said?" She bellowed- Elliott, he was hiding in the closet- And Susie, when she found him- she'd start pulling on his hair-

Again, the next day- Elliott wanted to see his friend Tina again- even though his mother insisted that he was not allowed to go over to her house anymore- (Elliott did not listen to his

mother) - so he tried to sneak around the back way and go through the garage area- and that's when Elliott tripped over and fell on broken glass- (of course it was a seven up pop bottle!) Elliott lifted up his shirt and saw a big hole in his stomach- Elliott was worried- he hurried home immediately! He showed his mother Pearl his tragically piercing wound- Pearl thought Elliott was teasing and thought it was jelly on his tiny little belly- but it certainly was not! Pearl screamed in horror! And just as she was going to call the ambulance- her older son James (unaware of the incident!) Traveled all the way in his friend's car from college, (about three hundred miles up north- not a moment too soon) - they came driving down the big hill- (boy what timing) - boy what luck! They rushed little Elliott into the car and raced Elliott straight to Memorial Hospital! (It was extremely critical- and very close that day- James and his friend, good thing that they made the trip back home)-

Elliott stayed in the hospital for the next seven days; he was terrified of needles- Elliott is trying to out run the nursing staff- and trying not to get pricked in the finger by a needle- the doctor and nursing staff getting prepped for giving Elliott a shot.

After Elliott was released from the hospital- Pearl took Susie and him to a great big department store. Mom would always take Susie and Elliott downtown every other weekend- they would go out and eat at all different kinds of restaurants- Pearl was always good to them- She even gave them an allowance (that's how Elliott bought all of his records- like "The Jackson Five") - he loved going to the record store- to pick out his music- even The Osmans- one bad apple-

There were toys and clothes and all kinds of cool items there* (at the department store)- everywhere Elliott looked (he was so excited)- (Elliott sees a big tan colored horse-about the size of his mother's hands)- Elliott, why he even became lost Downtown in the winter time (by himself) Elliott wondered off (while his mother and sister were shopping- Elliott is always up to no good- that's how he got lost) (checking out the manikins- looking up under their skirts)- when Elliott turned around, he could not find his mother or sister, so Elliott decided to walk home (on his own) in the cold, cold snow with no winter jacket on- (his mom and his sister are now franticly looking for Elliott) and that's when a cab driver approached Elliott and asked him if he needed a ride home, even as young as Elliott was, he refused the ride home, and he did make it home safely- no sooner than a few moments later, came Pearl and Susie! Guess Elliott was very lucky that day!

(NEW BEGINNING)

*Elliott was in school and did very well in all of his classes- he was an incredibly fast runner- (in fact his big cousin Roy use to make bets on him all the time, against a lot of the older children, and of course Elliott would win!)

Even though, the big kids would pick on him because he was so small and different.

(Elliott in class- was always being chased- and always winning races) The big day came when Elliott finally invited his family to watch him race- (some of his family members were in the crowd interacting and anticipating) when it came time to race, a few other kids, secretly made a plan-they were going to cheat- (they knew Elliott was a threat,) so they decided that they would leave the starting line a little sooner than everybody else- (their plan, it almost work)- until, Elliott protested to the judge, the judge- he re-considered the situation and awarded Elliott first place! You see- Elliott never lost a race before and that one, was a close one for Elliott- Simply put, running meant a lot to Elliott- It seemed to be a beautiful day after all- so Elliott asked his mother if he could walk home from school- (that was a big mistake)- some of the kids that were trying to cheat at the race earlier were still hanging around (along with one of the older brothers of one of the kids)- they saw Elliott, and wanted to catch him- teach him a lesson and beat him up- Elliott saw the kids heading towards him and he started to run, and Elliott- he did get away! Elliott was so relieved and happy- he started to laugh and smile- right at that same time Elliott was so busy enjoying his victory, there happened to be another group of kids (playing dice- around the back of the school) they were interacting, one of the younger boys: (NAMED ANDREW- seemed a bit too young to be hanging out with these older teens- as they were shooting dice the younger boy named Andrew, he was caught cheating- (Andrew threw the dice for the last time) so the older teens started to beat on the boy (real badly)- as the boy Andrew was lying there beat up from the older teens, for trying to cheat- the teens ran off* "COME ON, LET'S GO!"- (Just then Elliott came around the corner- smiling and laughing) - unaware of the young boy badly beaten up- right then, as the two (Elliott & Andrew) (seeing each other for the first time) - Elliott became afraid of the situation, and started to run! As the older kid Andrew was calling out for help- Elliott did not hear him* (a loud motorcycle and car were racing as they passed by)- and that is when the mean kid Andrew vowed: "IF IT IS THE LAST THING I'LL DO- I AM GOING TO GET THAT KID!"- (For laughing at me and running when I needed help)-

When Elliott got home from school that day the bigger kids said to him: "hey Elliott come over here and help us try out our new go-cart we just built!" Obviously Elliott was not afraid to try it- (he took it all the way up the big hill) (GULP!) Elliott would test the new go-cart (made out of wood) - and boy did he wipe out immediately! (Of course he was all right- and yes, the big kids, they all laughed at him)- (The boys finished the go-cart right before Elliott showed up)-

On Friday nights all the kids would go down to the neighborhood matinee and watch Kung Fu movies (including Bruce Lee flicks) they would get out after the show and pretend to fight, they had so much fun! (They were Kung Fu fighting) *However: Elliott's family moved quite a bit- When the big day came to move- the moving van showed up and all of the neighborhood kids came to play kickball, they all played like never before- all into the night! Elliott, he was on fire* like never before *too (almost as though they were trying to let him win) - but simply, Elliott was just smokin' hot that night! He had a blast that night!

Christmas time came and Elliott finally got what he'd wished for- a brand new shinny electric guitar! (He played a quick guitar solo)

Unfortunately, Elliott took his guitar apart, (and in no time flat!)- He play a funky sound, he broke his guitar!

Elliott somehow got a hold of his cousin' Roy's guitar- (the older cousin who use to bet on Elliott to win racing against the older kids) and Elliott, he had the knack for it- he loved his guitar and it was like magic! (Elliott was over at his cousin's house and asked to take the guitar home with him)

(TRANSITION)

(A little older Elliott)- in fact, Elliott loved his guitar so much that he started to skip school- besides he got tired of all of the bullies picking on him- (The ninth, tenth and eleventh graders were chasing Elliott again- Elliott runs one way and the kids go running another) That is one of the reasons; he prefers to play his guitar instead of being picked on-

Elliott played and played his guitar so much- he came up with a very unique sound of his own! Unlike any other sound before- (That's when Elliott decided to start up his own band) - they would practice in Elliott's garage- band members started to show up to the scene-

Elliott started working at a bar called Harold's- (cleaning floors) - since he was too young to hang out, he would go roller skating instead- and boy could he roller skate- and the girls went wild over his roller skating performances- after words they would all go hang out at McDonald's and when it became too late to catch the city bus home, they'd roller skate home (big sister Susie and Elliott would skate home together)

One night while Elliott was practicing with his band- the bass player decided to pull out some marijuana- Elliott was not too happy about it at first- but then the bass player decided to put it away-

Back at Elliott's work *one day, no one appeared to be around so Elliott went on stage and picked up the house guitar and (as he did not notice) - Harold the owner (a gangster) was in his back office on the phone having problems with his debt-

And Harold could not believe the sound he heard coming from out of that instrument out there! Harold wondered who the heck was playing so well. So he hurried and hung up the phone, because he needed to see whom this person was- (no one saw Harold watching)–

Harold was thinking up all kinds of ways to pack his house and Harold knew that Elliott would be the answer to all of his problems!

The very next day, Elliott had his roller skates on- (and was in a hurry to get to work that day- he had over slept) so he skated to: and snuck up behind the back of a city bus and hitched a ride- Rolling in the shadows-

So when Elliott finally arrived to work- Milo (one of Elliott's band members) was there too- Harold's bar was a little crowded that day, perhaps a meeting- Andrew was hiding in the shadows under his hat and wearing dark glasses- Elliott does not know him yet- Andrew had a tattoo- He discover that Elliott was there that's when he started working out his plan for Elliott- (but nothing big yet) So Milo and Elliott were in the back of the bar in one of the storage rooms and there was a great big guitar amp stacked up on a shelf back there- and Elliott bet Milo five dollars if he cranks the amplifier up and plugs in the guitar (back here)- he will play it awfully loud! Milo took the bet - So Elliott plugged up the guitar (that was back there) and cranked up the amp- at first nothing happened- then Milo said to Elliott: "hey man, what's that smell?" The two looked at each other and suddenly- "BOOM!!" That amp, it did make a noise! (No wonder it was back there) – should Elliott pay for the amplifier?

The next day, Elliott's band was practicing in Elliott's garage and it was starting to rain- (And comes Kevin - walking down the alley)- (Another thug who owes money to people)- Kevin heard the band playing and was mesmerized by the sound of Elliott's guitar- What Kevin didn't know that day was- Elliott was in a bad mood- the band was starting to get to him- Elliott was getting tired of their sound- Elliott needed a better sound- he would play a lot of wild tones on his guitar in between his guitar riffs- Kevin thought to himself- (man if I could get this band to sign- (especially this guitar player) I could be filthy rich!)- (He's pissed off)! - You see Kevin owed money to Harold and Mickey-

(And yes, Mickey was a gangster too)-

The night came- (it was somewhat a little strange that evening, there was a chill in the air)- Elliott decided to wander off and take a walk, (so he could try and figure out his dilemma, about his bands' sound)- (by himself down a dark alley) all of sudden two men came out of the darkness and started to chase Elliott- Elliott tripped and fell to the ground* and as Elliott rolled up on to his feet- Elliott spun around and kicked one of the men in his face! Right as Elliott came around from his first kick- Elliott immediately jumped up and kicked the other guy right into his jaw! As Elliott landed on to his feet- he looked up and notice that the two men where knock out cold on to the ground! "All that practicing Kung Fu- really paid off!" (Elliott thought to himself) as Elliott started to run; and when he finally ran out of breath, he just walked* and that's when he met a strange woman- (Who's that lady?) She was attractive-seductive and very sexy- she was walking her little pooch (named Wishes) (Elliott thought to himself again) "boy I must be in the wrong neighborhood!" Elliott could not resist the young girl's beauty- (he talked some smooth dialog) so he asked her back to his garage- and for the first time Elliott smoked marijuana and they made love all through the night! –

Her name was: Rainbow- and Elliott actually enjoyed the marijuana and of course he enjoyed Rainbow too- what a Heat Wave that was, always and forever remembered.

A couple of days went by and before anyone could say anything the police showed up at Elliott's house and wanted to bring him in for questioning- about the assault that occurred a couple of nights ago- Elliott was identified and because this was Elliott's first offence, the judge gave Elliott the option to either go to jail or enlist into the army- Now since Elliott was still yet a minor, Pearl (Elliott's mother) thought that would be the best thing for her young boy- so Elliott got himself an Army recruiter and took all the necessary requirements to enlist and before you knew it Elliott all of a sudden "was in the Army!"

Elliott was stationed at Fort Jackson: South Carolina and thought he would make a good try at it- the first thing Elliott noticed was a pretty young Sergeant- and thought to himself "boy this is going to be great"! The night came; everybody was in their bunk for the night- all of a sudden out of nowhere the lights came on! There was a big commotion, high-ranking soldiers were banging on lockers and trashcans and men were ordering: ALL RIGHT EVERYBODY UP! UP! UP! Elliott got up and his unit was ordered to load all the buses that were lined up out front- (Elliott was on the bus falling asleep) –

Before anyone could say a word Elliott's unit was standing in a line in Georgia:

Fort Benning 197 infantry! Elliott could not believe his eyes! He was devastated and all of the high ranks were talking trash and trying to intimidate the young soldier- The first chance Elliott got, he took, and he tried to call his Army recruiter and was told by the recruiter: "there is nothing I can do for you boy"- Elliott felt betrayed, bamboozled and had to come up with a solution to his dilemma- The next morning, Elliott was tired, he snuck under his bunk and they were looking for him- (he finally showed up) and one of his fellow soldiers said to him: "Elliott, you've got a roach on your head man!" Elliott immediately whisked it away! Another time, Elliott was in the chow line and he had some problems trying to do an "about face" – Elliott's Sergeant became angry with him and pulled out his pistol (GULP!)(It all seemed to be in slow motion) And asked Elliott to try it again- this time, in all the world of history, (by far) this was the most perfect "about face" you would ever have laid your eyes on! "That's it!" (Elliott thought to himself),"I'm getting out of here!" - So he tried a medical tactic, let's see: "I will dip my cigarette with a chemical and it will show up on x-ray"- Damn! Didn't work- he tried to act a little crazy, but nope, that didn't work either (in fact it almost made things worse for him)- Elliott even thought about shooting himself in the foot- nope, that wasn't a good idea- finally Elliott had one more plan- it had to work- Elliott simply stated that he was only sixteen years old and he lied to get in the Army- The Army put Elliott through a whole bunch a raggamaroo test and yes, Elliott was finally going to go home! (Elliott was walking through the airport) *Elliott has on: Army hat with sergeant stripes, army socks, and black shoes- black clothes (rayon material parachute pants along with/member's only shirt and with Army brass- Not to mention: top secret documents- (in his hands)

(THE VERY NEXT MONTH)

Elliott called up everybody- and he also went back to work at Harold's- this time Harold approached Elliott and asked: "if he would like to perform in his bar?" At first Elliott was stunned with the question- then Elliott was over whelmed with enthusiasm- he became excited- Then Elliott replied- "why yes- of course- I would be honored to play here at your place of business Harold- when can me and my band start?"- Harold replied-"oh no I just want you to play with my house band only"- Now Elliott did not want to play with these old men- they were way too old- (it wasn't Elliott's style)- so he had to tell Harold *no, he had to respectfully decline- (which Elliott really didn't want to do. Elliott kind of new that there was something bad, shifty or shady about Harold) so Elliott had asked if he could just finish his cleaning, and Elliott (he just walked away) - Now Harold on the other hand- he was Furious! (But did not show it)-

Back to rehearsal- with the band- Elliott had a different attitude that day- Milo said: "hey I know where we can go and start recording our songs for free"- that's when the group went into the studio that day and recorded- they acted like a bunch of fools, they were not serious about their music- they had girls there- they were smoking marijuana- Elliott just about had enough again!

Elliott was on his way to work- (this time he was walking- he was frustrated) Elliott ran into Kevin (for the first time) Kevin claimed he could make a big colossal deal out of Elliott's group! And make Elliott famous- if Elliott would sign the back of Kevin's funky business card- Elliott signed- Elliot didn't know any better- "the heck with it!"

(Elliott thought to himself)-

So Elliott was walking with Kevin to go check out the new place where Elliott's band was going to play- on the way they lit up some marijuana to celebrate their new business deal and that's when the cops started following them! Elliott and Kevin started to run; they ran so fast, that they got away!

Elliott and Kevin made it over to the new club Mickey's just in time- Elliott got on the phone to tell Milo about the new deal he got them- but Milo was in the recording studio and he could not get there- so Elliott was on his own- he went up on stage anyway and started to play his guitar (on his own) - Elliott was marvelous! He sounded great! He was terrific! Mickey (the club owner) immediately wanted to make things happen for Elliott- Kevin was off the hook with Mickey- But Mickey was not off the hook with Harold- And Harold- he happened to be at Mickey's club that night, watching- it seems you can't do anything without Harold finding out about it-

Later on, Kevin was happy and became too drunk- he needed to step out into the alley to have a smoke and urinate- all of a sudden-

Some headlights turned on and Harold and two goons stepped out of the car- still in the back seat was sitting Andrew- Harold was furious with Kevin and wanted to know why Elliott Jay is playing over at Mickey's? Kevin was terrified and tried to keep his cool-

He didn't have much to say, but he was sorry and said: "you can buy his contract from me"- now Harold wanted his money from Kevin- and didn't think that he should have to pay for Elliott's contract- Kevin said that he didn't have any money for Harold- so Harold told his two goons to work Kevin over-

Later that night, Elliott is with his new girlfriend Rainbow (in the garage) Elliott is getting ready to perform a strange guitar ritual- "breaking guitars"- Rainbow is thinking (to herself) she should probably buy Elliott a brand new guitar tomorrow-

They make love-

(The next day) Milo and Elliott get together-and they need money for the big night at Mickey's- Milo introduces Elliott to one of his thug buddies Corey- So Elliott and Corey ran up to Kmart to try and steal some merchandise to get some marijuana and cash for the evening- Corey gets his score- Elliott's a little nervous- but he try's- just as soon as Elliott gets to the two front doors with the merchandise- Elliott feels a hand on his back/he is being chased by two security guards!

Elliott starts to make a run through the Kmart parking lot in broad daylight! Across the busy intersection, Elliott ran three blocks through the neighborhood complex he sees a little boy, looks at him and quietly says "shush" and rolls under a back patio fence- as the guards run past him, and he did slip away!

(That evening)- Elliott was with his band in the garage- getting ready for the night's performance- Rainbow showed up with a smokin' hot new red guitar! The band was ready for the night!

The band showed up at Mickey's and before they could even set up- Harold was there- with two of his body guards and regretted to inform them that: "this show is canceled because your contract belongs to me now boy!"

(FADE TO BLACK)

Elliott is in a slump and now has to figure out what his next move is going to be- Elliott is walking and smoking- and has his guitar on his back- Elliott hears somebody speaking to him from a limo- kind of a good looking and well put together young man- the young man's name is Andrew (he is now in-to play): Andrew asks: "do you play well?" "If so come with me," Elliott says: "by now I have nothing to lose"- so Elliott got in to the car and went with Andrew- Andrew and Elliott were being chauffeured to Andrew's place-

Elliott arrives at the young man's house and was shocked! Elliott finally found someone who played like he wanted and could really appreciate the young man's talents they hit it off! (The sun is beginning to set) Then Andrew asks the question:

"do you remember a long time ago when we were kids and you saw a young boy badly beaten up- and you laughed and ran away?" Elliott thought about it for a moment and started to worry; Andrew say's "try and remember!"- Elliott say's "yes, I think I do remember now- how do you know about that- was that, was that you man?" Andrew was starting to get upset and answered: "yes, man that was- that was me- You're lucky that I don't paste your face all over these walls man-

Why did you laugh at me, why did you laugh and run away- why did you do it?" Elliott now realizes that this is the mean kid that use to hang out with the older teens and now probably wants to get even with him- Elliott thought about it and truthfully answered back-

"Man, I was always being chased by kids, (all the time) and now I remembered that day when I had my family there for the big race and these kids; these kids they tried to cheat me out of the big race- and at first the judge gave them the trophy, but then I complained because anyone could see that they took off running way before they were supposed to- the judge didn't make a big deal about it until I spoke up- (Andrew's reply): "so what's that got to do with what I just asked you punk?") "Hold on, please- let me finish, so then the judge awarded me with the big win- and later on that day, when I was walking home- they all tried to gang up on me- and that's when I ran and I got away, I was so happy* that I was smiling and laughing and that's when I saw you and made a run for it, I was scared- I'm sorry for any misunderstanding we ever had with each other* over that crazy stupid messed up day."- Andrew thought about it for a second and he felt in his heart that Elliott was telling the truth, and that Elliott meant no harm to Andrew. Andrew decided that he wanted to have Elliott as a true friend- So, after a while they spoke and got to know each other better-

(PAUSE)

Andrew was driving Elliott home in one of his fancy new cars, and out from nowhere, a car sped up to them, and was trying to ram in to them! It became a car chase! These hostile men started shooting at Andrew and Elliott, and Andrew asked Elliott: "if he knew how to drive?" And Elliott said: "hell yes!"- So they made a quick switch- as Andrew started shooting at the car, that was chasing and shooting at them- Andrew shot out one of the tires and the hoodlums car spun out of control and crashed right in to the ditch and immediately started on fire- that's when Andrew told Elliott to hurry up and turn around and head back to the car- Andrew and Elliott pulled up to the car and there were three men inside and they were all trapped and Andrew asked: "who sent you?"

I said: "who sent you!?" Andrew yelled! Finally one of the men said: "Harold, it was Harold who sent us"- Andrew said to Elliott (as a police siren was faint in the distance) "let's get out of here!"- It appeared that two of the men died, but the one who told on Harold was pleading for help and Andrew and Elliott had to get out of there fast! And fast they did!

Elliott left Milo and his band behind and decided to play with this new group- the new group Elliott played with had lots and lots of money- they would practice their own music in a private warehouse space- The group had women, cars and everything you could imagine- but there was still the issue of Harold-

What were Elliott and Andrew going to do about this Harold situation? Elliott decided to talk to his new found group about his contract problem and they said let's just go over there and talk to him and see if we all can work something out with the man- Elliott was relieved that the group was on his side- So the group headed over to Harold's place, and of course Harold was there-

Elliott wanted to get out of his contract with Harold badly- so Elliott proposed an offer to perform for one night only (with no pay) and the band will play at Mickey's club, after that the group will give Harold ten percent a week for one year- so Harold agreed to it-

Elliott's new band had the place packed, Milo and the old band was there- the place was jumpin' and it was ready to explode in there! The music played-

The band performed greatly! Better than anybody could have ever imagined- Harold made so much money that night- HE HAD TO HAVE THE GROUP COME BACK FOR MORE! (After seeing all that money in his hands) Harold had no intentions on ever sharing his money with the group-

Or anybody else! Remember, Harold, he owed money too! (But that was not the deal they made with one another)- Harold wanted Elliott's group to continue to perform at his bar- but Elliott and Andrew should have known that they could not do business with Harold. Later on, Harold had a meeting with his cronies and they decided that they were going to kidnap Rainbow to make Elliott and his band stay and play more nights-

(On the phone, Harold was talking to Elliott) Elliott didn't know what to do- so Elliott told his new friend (Andrew) about his situation and Andrew had a plan- you see Andrew came from a family of thugs too and he was about to deal with Harold (on his own terms)

(Rainbow was safely tucked away)- KEVIN (all beat and patched up) TALKING TO ANDREW & ANDREW'S TWO GOONS- OF COURSE ELLIOTT IS UNAWRE OF THEIR PLANS!

(The plan was set in place/it was late, late night)- they watched and waited for Harold to show up to his bar- Harold finally showed- Kevin approached Harold by distracting him- at first Harold was upset to see Kevin, "what are you doing here Kevin? I thought I got rid of you, you dirt bag?" Then Kevin answered: "I got your money boss"- Harold, he liked the sound of that! That's when the two men came out of the darkness and abducted Harold- they shoved him in to his car- then they took Harold to a remote location- and let him know that if you don't let Rainbow go- not only will you be out of a bar- but Harold, you will be out of your life as well- Harold was so surprised and wondered how the hell did they know about his plan- Harold had no choice but to make the call- Andrew found out were Rainbow was by tracking Harold's call (Andrew had one of his goons planted in at Harold's camp) as soon as they got Rainbow out of there- the police showed up mysteriously and rounded up the rest of Harold's goons and Rainbow was released to Elliott- and Andrew decided to make Harold an offer he could not refuse- by sending Harold packing- Elliott's group took over Harold's bar- Mickey now owes Elliott-

Elliott's group ended up playing that night (not to mention they own the bar now) and Harold is off somewhere trying to figure out what the hell went wrong!

THE END!!!???

http://www.myspace.com/kurtjxxx

This is based on a true story- Where is Elliott Jay now? He might be sitting right next to you.

Some Music written by: kurtj c2009 = other music by:

Dirty Nephew Productions*
PRESENTS:

"That Kid" - Part Two (VENGENCE)

Written by kurtj c2009

*Harold went in hiding (down in Miami) he is now sitting at a bar- drinking and gathering up his thoughts- he is also running out of money, and fast, the reason Harold went down to Miami is because Milo told him about a cousin that lives there; and owns a bar- The cousin with a couple of beautiful women wrapped around his arms-

Now Milo's cousin knows about a treasure that is buried somewhere in the Miami water- and the reason Milo's cousin has no interest in it whatsoever; is because Milo's cousin is bound to a wheelchair, and he has no desire to go through the trouble of finding the gold and he also suspects that it just may be a myth or a legend even- but one thing is for sure is; Harold and Milo are determined to prove this cousin wrong. The two, they are ready to find the gold at all cost, no matter what! (Milo was talking to Harold, back in Minnesota after the amplifier blew up. (The fact that it wasn't mentioned until now is, when Harold jumped up after the explosion he came running) during that incident Harold had a meeting with Milo, everybody else was too busy ducking and hiding on account of; they all thought it was something a lot more serious than an amplifier going off)- *Milo also has a conversation with Kevin and tells him about the cousin who knows where there may be some gold buried in Miami as well- (Milo was always talking with Kevin behind Elliott's back)- and Harold also tells Milo: "when I send for you – you'd better get your ass down here- and you'd better get down here fast boy!"

"And keep your mouth shut, don't say anything to anybody about this, and I mean it Milo!"(Obviously, Milo did not listen, he told Kevin)-

(NOTE: KEVIN WAS ALWAYS HAVING SECRET MEETINGS- AND MILO COULD NEVER FIGURE OUT WHERE KEVIN WAS GETTING ALL OF HIS DOPE FROM- MILO'S CREW WAS NOT SURE, BUT THEY MAY SUSPECT THAT KEVIN COULD POSSIBLY BE AN UNDER COVER FED)*

(BACK IN MINNESOTA)

Elliott and Andrew are having problems working together with their music- they are trying to run Harold's old bar- but they can't seem to agree upon; whether they should perform more* because Andrew wants to get into selling more drugs (to keep the bar afloat)- but Elliott thinks they can do much better, by performing more of Elliott's songs, and selling more of his music-

(BACK IN MIAMI)

Milo is trying to look cool with Kevin on the plane- Milo is being a big jerk to the stewardess; and in the back ground there appears to be an undercover fed- (but we are not sure yet)- the plane lands in Miami and they all meet up at Milo's cousin's bar- and *that's where the hunt for gold begins- (Kevin shows up with Milo and Harold isn't too pleased about that)- "Ok Milo, here we go again, you must be trying to get on my bad side already, aren't you?" Harold says to Milo- "Why did you bring this stupid ass nincompoop Kevin all the way down here to Miami with you, you jack-ass?" "If you had a clue, you would know that Kevin does not belong here with us- at all!" Harold turns to ask Kevin: "Kevin what in the hell are you doing here?" Right before Kevin had a chance to open his mouth, Harold says: "Never mind I'll ask you, Milo?" Milo answers back at Harold and says: "Kevin financed me to get here and after what we've been through; I know you can trust this man by now" "Why should I be able to trust Kevin?" Harold asked Milo- Milo answers again and says: "because when Elliott and / "HEY, WOAH, DO NOT MENTION THAT MOTHER FR'S NAME TO ME!" Yelled Harold-

(BACK IN MINNESOTA)

(It was a night performance) and it happened to be a nice size crowd that evening- the group was really rocking hard* and it was time for a break- now Andrew went back to his dressing room, and Elliott was Smiling because he knew the crowd was feeling the music that night- suddenly, Andrew starts to snort some coke- Elliott replies: "HEY MAN, WHAT THE HECK! I thought you were just going to sell that stuff, not use it?" Andrew tells Elliott to go away and he'll be right out for their next performance-

(MEANWHILE, BACK IN MIAMI)

"But you asked me to explain," Said Milo- "alright then, go ahead bone-head Milo, explain yourself, explain yourself to me please!" Said Harold, as he was grinding on his teeth- "Ok then" as Milo continued- "so when those two chumps back in Minnesota where trying to take over and run your bar- me and this dude Kevin here were supplying them with some of those goodies, and Kevin was making most of the money (not me) - and the last time I checked, things weren't going so great for them two clowns" (With Andrew and Elliott)" – "Yes, yes! Now that's what I like to hear my little brother" - says Harold- (as he joyfully smiles)-

It looks like Milo, Kevin and Harold, end up purchasing the map from Milo's cousin after all- and the crew of three went down to rent them a boat– the three men headed out- in search for the gold; and as they set sail, for the treasure, they were starting to realize (something to themselves)- that this voyage may not be all fun and games- and as they all looked at one another* suddenly, a twin engine Cessna flew by- (over the crew)- they didn't really think anything of it- but if you look closely, you will notice that the guy inside the twin engine is the same person who was flying on the plane earlier with Milo and Kevin)- the crew, they'd better hope that they all have enough gear- Harold was starting to order Milo around, because Harold was so use to being the boss- (and it felt good to him - for a change) and Milo decided; since he put this operation together, he was going to tell Kevin what to do, after; all Milo was the one who came up with the whole Idea)- but it seemed as though things were probably going to get a lot worse before they get any better. Looks like the crew may be heading for a great big disaster-

(BACK IN MINNESOTA)

As Elliott was headed back out to the stage, he was ready to perform another song- Andrew decided to leave, he jumped into his limo and drove off- Elliott was use to running the band on his own- and right as Elliott was about ready to start performing-

(BACK IN MIAMI)

Harold and his new crew finally ended up near a small cave, and they anchored; it was a good thing Milo happened to be a good swimmer- and as Milo put on his swim gear,

He started to submerge under water-

He looked everywhere and according to the map they should have been right over the gold; but it appeared that the crew was having problems locating the treasure- they just couldn't locate anything, they could not get their bearings right- the crew was starting to get a little restless-

(BACK IN MINNESOTA)

As Andrew rode off and left Elliott behind, Andrew went searching for some more drugs, and Andrew was starting to get a little bit out of control- even his Limo driver was starting to become concerned- *meanwhile on stage Elliott was starting to perform another song - the crowd loved his performance, but a few of the fans were yelling for Andrew- (Elliott was starting to feel the pressure)-

(BACK IN MIAMI)

(Harold's crew was getting aggravated with one another)- Milo's equipment was starting to malfunction- suddenly, there became arguments with one another, the men were overwhelmed, hungry and just plain tired- Milo, he was already tired of diving, period- and it was beginning to become very late-

Milo said: "look if we can't find the gold, then what are we going to do about all of our expenses?" "You know there has been a lot of money spent out here already?" "How are we supposed to make good?" Kevin told Milo to shut up and stop complaining- (the two immediately exchanged foul words) Milo became very angry with Kevin and proceeded to punch Kevin right in his face! Before you knew it, Milo and Kevin were going at it having a slugfest! The two were fighting harshly on the Voyager and Harold was doing his best to try and calm the two hooligan's down- but it came to no avail, as a gun went off!

(PAUSE)

And it appeared at first that Milo was shot-

(BACK IN MINNESOTA)

Andrew ended up finding one of his drug dealer's, (a Cuban dude called Gino, now Andrew was at Gino's house) and Gino asked Andrew if he has ever heard of this new drug called free-basing, and if he would like to give it a try? Andrew said; that he was not familiar with the drug, and the dealer wanted Andrew to try some- (free on the house) and since the dealer knew that Andrew's money was good, if all went well, they could have a very lucrative relationship together-

(PAUSE)

It was night fall, the show was over for the evening, Elliott was at home with Rainbow- Elliott was frustrated with what was going on with Andrew and his world, Elliott was trying to explain to Rainbow his situation, but Rainbow had something else in mind, she needed to tell Elliott-

(BACK IN MIAMI)

Kevin who was the one who was shot (accidentally by Milo) - Harold became extremely angry- and he says to Milo: "do you realize, what you have-just-done?" "What in the hell is wrong with you man?" "What were you thinking dude?" "How could you ever get so sloppy?" "You know we did need him man- right?" Milo just stood there looking like a fool in the rain- Harold continued: "well, aren't you going to say anything to me?" "I thought you didn't like him anyways man, I thought I did you a favor" was the first damn thing that came out of Milo's ignorant mouth-

(BACK IN MINNESOTA)

Andrew took a toke off the new drug and kicked back and relaxed-(Andrew loved it) – Meanwhile, Elliott was trying to tell Rainbow about the problems he was having with Andrew,

Rainbow abruptly said to Elliott: "Elliott, I am pregnant?" Elliott was surprised; and calmly ordered his young beautiful woman over to him- as he whisked her gently, he was full of tears-

(BACK IN MIAMI)

Milo roared back at Harold* and stated: "man, he was a good for nothing- besides, I owed him lots of money and he was always holding that against me; (every damn chance he'd get*) - and I just couldn't take it anymore, I was just sick of it!" All of that hustling and running around for him- back and forth, to and from and he still was a bum!" "So good ridings to bad rubbish!" That's what I always say!"- And Harold answered back to Milo, saying: "You stupid good for nothin' fool; I hope you don't expect me to carry all the gold when we do find it!!" "Besides, what are we supposed to do with the man's body Milo?"- "I guess we'll have to dump it, over board?" Milo said- so the two men wrapped and chained Kevin's body, and threw it over board, in the rain.

(FADE TO BLACK)

It's now dark, and Milo is starting to complain to Harold again: "Where's the gold man?" I'm tired of being out here!" "There isn't any damn gold out here man- I bet my cousin was full of crap" "I even bet he played us both for fools!" wait, wait hold on, Harold said: "now what did you just say, you little piece of crap?!" Milo said:

"I said I bet my cousin must have played us both for fools; you dumb ass sucker ass!" Harold was already furious and told Milo: "you know what Milo?" "You'd better just shut the hell up and stop your damn lying and whining!"-

"Now get your stupid little lazy ass down in the water and stop talking trash to me, you stupid little imbecile- (son of a bitch'n, whore!") "As much crap that I've put up with you today-

Boy, don't you test me no more!" Milo became very angry, but he decided to stay real quiet and he kept his cool; as Harold pulled out his gun and said to Milo: "now look son, why don't you just try and take one more dive and we'll hope for the best this time alright?"

And we'll see if there's something down there- ok?" "Come on Milo, one more time, what do you say?" Then Milo replied: "ok, all right then sure"- (as Harold rolled his eyes)

(BACK IN MINNESOTA)

(Elliott and Rainbow) "I think maybe we should get married," says Rainbow- Elliott thought about it for a second and says: "you know what, that would be nice babe, I know a guy who owns a record label in Phoenix, and he would love to hear my demo- baby girl." "You mean you don't have to be here stuck with Andrew anymore?" Rainbow replies- "Yes doll, we could go and travel all over the country just like we always talked about, but first we have to deal with that little bun you've got in the oven, Hun." Says Elliott-

(BACK IN MIAMI)

Milo dives into the water, (one last time)- (now Milo was down there for a real good long time), and Harold was starting to wonder if Milo would ever come up- finally Milo came up and said Anxiously: "I think I might have found something down there!"

Milo had spotted something down there, and Harold, he was starting to feel real good about it inside, and he gave Milo the big boom-claw and as they lowered it down

(Along with Milo attached to it)- Milo continued to look and look again- AND YES FINALLY- THEY DID FIND SOMETHING DOWN THERE! IT WAS A GREAT BIG OLD LARGE RUSTY CHEST!!! The now two men, hoisted up the chest and placed it on the deck of the boat, and as they gazed at it in fulfillment- (the large old decrepit chest)- Harold wanted to open up a bottle of champagne and make a toast- (but Milo was thinking about knocking Harold over the head with it,)- but instead, he decided to keep his cool once again- "might as well keep this old sucker around 'til we get back to shore:" Milo thought to himself. They toasted with one another, to the good life.

(BACK IN MINNESOTA)

Andrew really enjoyed the new drug so much, that he decided to invest in quite a bit of it- Andrew was on his way back to the bar and was feeling pretty good about his new investment, he figured that; this is going to work, he will have people eating out of the palm of his hands- he also thought that him and Elliott were going to write some more music together, when he gets back to the bar-

(BACK IN MIAMI)

Harold used a crow bar to pry open the chest- and when they finally opened up the old chest, they found exactly what they were hoping for- GOLD! Old precious coins and jewels- how lucky they were! They both thought to themselves that they could hardly imagine it; that they truly found pure gold!

(BACK IN MINNESOTA)

Elliott kissed Rainbow, and headed back to the bar to see if Andrew had arrived yet, (Elliott played some music in his van- and they both pulled up at the bar; right around the same time- Elliott was a little upset and concerned and asked Andrew why he never showed up to perform; Andrew said to Elliott:

"Forget about that man, I got something that will knock your socks off kid!" Elliott was thinking: "ok, now what's this going to be?" Andrew said: "come on inside, you've got to check this shit out!" The two, they went in-

(BACK IN MIAMI)

Harold and Milo were preparing to head back to civilization- and it was beginning to rain a bit harder now- Harold said "it looks like it's going to be a big one-" Milo didn't care, all he could think about was that treasure. The two men they prepared for sail, and that's when a huge storm started to approach them. It started to come down hard, there was lightning and thunder, the wind was blowing strong! The Voyager was rocking hard, back and forth; the two men were beginning to panic- "what are we going to do with all of this weight we've got on board?" Asked Milo, hysterically- "the boat is filling up with water fast! What in the hell are we going to do?" Milo cried again- "Man, we're starting to sink!" Harold screams: "start throwing all of the heavy gear over board, hurry, hurry, hurry!"

(BACK IN MINNESOTA)

Andrew and Elliott were kicking back in their (back-office) talking about their future, and Andrew was trying to explain to Elliott about the new drug that he just discovered and purchased. Elliott wasn't at all that convinced or enthusiastic about it- so Andrew prepared a toke for Elliott to smoke, but Elliott wasn't really that interested; and Andrew was getting a little ticked off because Elliott didn't want to see eye to eye with Andrew; but Elliott was still trying to convince Andrew about their music. Andrew was still set on selling those drugs- Andrew said the hell with it and decided to take another toke of his new found drug. Again, as Elliott was trying to explain to Andrew about Rainbow being pregnant- Elliott decided not to say anything about it that night-

(BACK IN MIAMI)

Nothing seemed to work from keeping that boat from sinking- Harold wanted to throw the chest over board to save his own life (he was terrified!) He tried to think of everything else possible to keep that stupid idea out of his mind- the two men were yelling and screaming and cursing and wishing, wishing that they've never set sail on that water that cursed water! Suddenly Harold yelled to Milo: "we're going to have to throw the chest over board!" "Oh no were not!" Screamed back Milo-

"We're going to have to do something or else were going to die damn it!" Once again Harold yelled: "How about if we shovel some of it out and over?" Franticly suggested Milo-

"Ok, let's do it then"- says Harold- the two men proceeded with dumping their harsh dreams over board* and finally, it was starting to work! The Voyager started stay afloat better and the men were finally heading closer to the shore. Harold got on his CB radio (hoping that it would work) ordering Milo's cousin to send a crew to meet them, and he will take care of everything else-

(BACK IN MINNESOTA)

The next day, Andrew is really falling in love with his new drug, and he is starting to use it more than he wants to sell it. In fact: he is starting to owe more money to the Cubans, and some of the equipment is starting to disappear. Elliott confronts Andrew about his drug use and some of the equipment that is beginning to disappearing. "So Andrew, Elliott asks: what happened to one of my guitars?" With a bold look on Elliott's face- Andrew answers back: "oh I accidentally broke it, and then I put it in the guitar repair shop" "how in the hell did you do that when you barely even play the damn thing?" Elliott replies. Then Elliott asks Andrew again: say Andrew, did you happen to see my keyboard module?" "Nope, says Andrew. "Well then, just what in the hell is going on with you anyways man, asks Elliott" "dude, lay off my back!" As Andrew gets up and walks away. As Elliott looks at Andrew walking away, Elliott decides to call it quits-

Elliott starts to pack up all of the rest of his equipment; he takes it out to his van and proceeds to bring his entire gear home with him-

(BACK IN MIAMI)

Harold and Milo finally make it back to land- the first thing Milo does is jump out of the boat and kisses the dock! Harold says to him: "stop playing around fool and let's get the hell out of here!" As a small crew meets the two, Harold and Milo are now on their way to paradise! They went to the hotel Legume, and were treated like royalty! They ordered room service by the dozen! They had women in their suite; the skies were no limit for the two gents! Harold says, as the men were starting to become intoxicated; and overwhelmingly ecstatic: "Milo my friend, I think we need to go back to Minnesota and take care of some business there!" "What do you mean boss man?" Asks Milo- Harold answers back (without hesitation) "You know there are two clowns back there who I would love to deal with-

On a personal level" "I don't know if that's a good idea Harold" Milo responds hesitantly. "Then you tell me boy, what should we do with my bar and my old friends, not to mention*

ALL THIS DAMN MONEY WE GOT NOW FOOL!" "I guess I see your point Harold" Milo answers respectfully. "All right now then, everybody out; us men, we've got some packing and planning to do here, we're going back to Minnesota!" Harold and his new crew of four men,

(Including Milo), are headed back to Minnesota-

(BACK IN MINNESOTA)

The feds are set up in a secret location, they are having a meeting* (Regarding- OPERATION HAROLD) - the agent, Harris is reporting to his commander, and states that agent Kevin Sims was last seen; when the undercover plane flew over the subjects in Miami- and has not been spotted since. Meanwhile, the FBI has information that Harold has a new crew and they are on their way back to Minnesota-

****
Elliott heads for home, and when he gets there- there are two men (the feds) that greet him, and want to ask him some questions-

Elliott does not have any information for the feds and they give him a card- Elliott gets inside his house and Rainbow asks him-"who were the two men outside?"

Elliott tells her that they were just Jehovah's witnesses and just left it at that-

(MEANWHILE)

Andrew is at the bar about to lock up and leave, just then; a couple of the Cuban men were wondering* when are they going to see their money? Andrew told them that his partner Elliott owed him a lot of money and they should have it within a couple of days; but the men weren't too happy about hearing that, they told Andrew that they didn't have a couple of days to wait, so they gave Andrew a verbal warning, that he had one day or else there coming back for him and Elliott- Andrew wasn't aware, but Harold was on the move, and already had two of his goon's watching Andrew - (parked outside)

Andrew heads over to Elliott's house to finally tell Elliott, what's really going on. Elliott becomes extremely angry and concerned he is worried about his family's safety and now he is confused. Elliott wanted to smoke some marijuana now, but Andrew suggested mixing some of the new drug with it- because it tastes so much better Andrew says. Rainbow walks into the room and Elliott asked her to go upstairs so him and Andrew can figure out some things- (Rainbows says she'll be back, she's going to go to the store- Elliott kisses her goodbye) - after Andrew rolled up the new drug for Elliott to first try, Andrew wanted to explain that they are in some serious danger- and Elliott took a toke of the new combination of drugs and asked: why to Andrew? What did Andrew do this time to get them in so much trouble? Andrew Explained that their lives were in danger and Elliott immediately asked about Rainbow, and Andrew said not to worry about her-

They don't know that she even exists- so Elliott felt at least relieved about that, and wanted to know more details about; what really was going on- Andrew told Elliott that he owes certain Cubans' a lot of money by tomorrow or else they are going to get it and get it good- Elliott was pissed off with Andrew and said that he can probably get the money from his dad, "but what good would that do for us- you're just going to get us in this predicament again, aren't you Andrew?"

Rainbow is at the store and she just bought her groceries and is now on her way out of the store, just then, two men came* one man came up from behind her and grabbed her; and ordered her into his car- where another man was waiting (and looking around) - Rainbow was terrified and the two men got a kick out of it and drove off- "where are you taking me?" The beautiful young pregnant Princess asked- "shut up bitch" Says one of the kidnappers; as he slaps her right in the face.

Elliott is more calmer now and tells his partner Andrew that this pot ain't all that bad- and wants more-

Rainbow ends up staring at the eyes of Harold, once again! And the poor girl cannot believe her eyes- "so, long time no sees; pretty lady"- Harold says as he continues: (Rainbow is scared) - "you know it's been a long time?" "And I've waited for this moment"- (as his goons are surrounded around the young beautiful girl; with grimacing faces) "don't touch me you fat pig!" (Rainbow pleads) Harold smacks her around, and draws blood- she looks up at him slowly-

Elliott calls up his dad Marlow and pleads with him for money, Marlow is very disappointed in his little boy Elliott and tells him that: "there's nothing that I can do for you anymore son" he tells his son Elliott, that he is on his own; as he hangs up on his boy. His father cries. Elliott was furious! And says to Andrew: "come on, let's go man, let's get out of here for now!" And the two leave. As both of them left and got into Elliott's van, a vehicle started following them- and the two; by now they know when someone is on their tail- so they gunned it and lost the car! "I wonder who in the hell was that?" Elliott asks- "I bet it was those Cuban dudes man" Said Andrew. "What about Rainbow man?" Says Elliott:

"I better head on back!" "Well, we are going to have to figure something out before tomorrow." Says Elliott- "Oh, you know what? I almost forgot" "There were some feds over at my house today-" says Elliott- "what did they want" asked Andrew franticly- "they asked me about Harold," "Harold?" Andrew says- " What did you say?" asks Andrew- "I told them I didn't know anything, and one of the guys handed me a card"- "a card!" Yelled Andrew- "why in the hell are you even talking to them man?" "I wasn't but"- "but what, you snitch?" "What?" "Why are you calling me a snitch man?" "'Cause, that's what you are you cream puff!" "Oh hell no" "Fine, then get out man!" "Bye!" "Bye yourself!" says Andrew, as he slams the door. (As Elliott drives off fast) he lights up what's left (in the ash tray) as he heads back home-

(ELLIOTT GOES HOME)

As Elliott returns to his house, he notices that the same type of car is parked nearby again- Elliott goes inside (and wonders where the hell Rainbow is?) Suddenly the phone rings- it is Harold- "Harold what the hell do you want from me now, and how did you get my phone number?" Elliott asks- "I got it from your sweet ass sexy lady"- Harold sings: "SEXY

LADY- SEXY MOMMA" "and let me tell you boy, she sure was sweet"- as Harold boast- "what do you mean was?" "And where the hell is my girl at- you F'n son of a bitch!" Elliott angrily asks- "I don't know, I guess you're just going to have to figure that one out for yourself, boy" Harold says- " I'll tell you what Elliott *boy, why don't you and your buddy Andrew meet me at (the old nuns warehouse in three hours no cops; and I will tell you where your precious little bitch is!" as Harold hangs up the phone and laughs, Elliott is in a daze and he doesn't know what to do- he can't count on Andrew anymore, he certainly can't depend on his dad Marlow either-

(FADE TO BLACK)

Elliott has no one to turn to on this one, he is beside himself; he starts going through his wallet to see if there is anybody or anything he can turn to for help- (Elliott is helpless and hopeless)-

As he is going through his wallet one last time, a card falls slowly to the floor- the card of an Agent-

(Special Agent Harris* of the FBI) Elliott is all out of options now, all he knows is that he isn't going to say anything about Andrew, and he wants his girl, he needs his Rainbow (that's for sure) that's it- that's all- as Elliott is running out of time, he hesitantly dials the number- at first no answer- then finally, Elliott's phone rings back, he answers immediately! It's Special Agent Harris with the FBI and Elliott has to explain that his precious woman Rainbow has been kidnapped by Harold and Harold wants to meet Elliott at a designated place at a certain time and soon! Agent Harris and his team meet up with Elliott and they go through all the details* as they start to head out-

-MEANWHILE,

Andrew is out of drugs and is on a rampage! As soon as Andrew gets to the bar there are some more Cuban men waiting for him- they lead Andrew into his bar and are considering taking over the joint- but Andrew is not that kind of man to back down, so the Cuban men decide to ruff Andrew up a little taste, BAM!

As Elliott and the feds are headed over to the hidden location, Elliott is really concerned about Rainbow and he is losing his temper- Special Agent Harris tells Elliott not to worry-

Andrew is being beat up real badly by these men, and as Andrew laid there (getting the shit kicked out of him)- he finds his little secret hiding place, where he keeps one of his gun - and slowly reaches for it he lets off a couple of shots, BING-BING! And he didn't miss his targets- Andrew was slow to get up; as he eased up (off the floor) to call his limo driver so he could come and help him out- just then as Andrew started to feel some relief, another gun shot went off! And this time it wasn't Andrew doing the shooting! As Andrew slowly fell back to the floor, he met the eyes of the Cuban boss* (the one he did business with)-

Elliott, Special Agent Harris and his hit squad, were already in position as Harold was hiding and had all of his goons set in place, Elliott yelled- "alright I'm here ass whole, where is she, where is my Rainbow?" Before anyone could say anything, a big light flashed on, CLICK- the horror; there laid the body of Rainbow! Elliott screamed in agony! He ran quickly to her body! He was furious! As he let his tears fall from his eyes to her bruised and battered body- just then, Harold came out slowly from the shadows and pointed his gun at Elliott- "damn, I was hoping that you would have brought your knuckle headed stupid ass boy Andrew"- Harold says eagerly- "why you dumb ass son of a bitch- you killed my girl, you mother fckr!" "She was all I had, she was my hope and dream, she was my, she was my angel!" As Elliott quietly cried out to Harold- "Well, you see- ain't much, I said there ain't too much that you can do about it now* boy, now is there?" Harold boldly states- "all right boys, grab him"- as Harold's lynch-mob grabbed Elliott- Elliott noticed a familiar face- "Milo, what the hell are you doing here with Harold?" Elliott asked desperately- "get'n paid fool- ha- ha- ha" - suddenly, the feds came on a loud speaker horn:

"HAROLD WASHINGTON JR., THIS IS THE FBI, YOU HAVE THREE MINUTES TO GIVE YOUR SELF UP!" Milo laughs: "ha-ha-ha, your name is Harold Jr." "Shut up Milo!! Harold says-

(PAUSE-BACK TO HAROLD/ELLIOTT)

"Damn punk, you called the feds on me, didn't you, you snitch?" asked Harold again- Just then Elliott spun out of his hold- (from one of the goons, and as Elliott was going to go straight for Harold, a gun went off! And Elliott fell to the floor! As soon as that shot went off, the feds moved in; they were having a gun battle, as poor Elliott laid there near Rainbow's body, Harold, somehow got away- but Milo got wounded and the other goons died-

It was a great big commotional crime scene* as several emergency vehicles were dispatched, Along with the TV and helicopter news reporting:

(DIALOG-ANCHOR WOMAN SPEAKS)-

"There was a big battle shoot out tonight at the old nuns' home, four people are dead and two are injured..."

(FADE TO BLACK)

Elliott is in the hospital wounded in bed, the doctor is there- "Elliott, I have some good news for you, your baby is in stable condition and we are hoping for a miracle"- Elliott is speechless, and falls back to sleep- it is now around midnight, and Elliott is just now waking up- as he opens his blurry eyes, he now sees Harold starring down at him! Harold is just about to put a pillow over Elliott's face, and that's when Agent Harris shows up! The two men are fighting as Harold gets the best of the Special Agent, Harold makes a quick run for it, and again, he gets away! "Are you all right Elliott?" Asks the Agent- Elliott is choking, and whispers: "yes, I'm ok" "good, 'cause we're going to have to place you in some kind of protective surveillance" says the Agent- "I better go check on your child"- the Agent says- as he calls for back up-

(GOING HOME)

Elliott and his child recover and are on their way home, they get out of the cab (Elliott is still in pain) the two go into the house where there are nothing but memory's- (ELLIOTT LOOKS AROUND, IT IS QUIET) As Elliott holds his child, he starts to cry again, and he kisses his little girl soft and gently. As he gingerly sets her on the bed- Elliott walks over to his dresser, he opens up his photo album looking at all of the concerts that he performed in, and his beloved beautiful precious Rainbow- as he sets the photo book down- and as he turns; POW!!! Harold punches him, in the face! Elliott falls to the floor~ the baby is crying now; he can hear vibrations and ringing his ears. He hears Rainbow's voice. "Oh hell no, not this time mother F'kr!" Elliott says to himself! Elliott happened to have a gun placed and ready, just for a moment like this- (for intruders,) and as he ran for it- KA'KICK!!! Harold got him good again, this time in the gut! Elliott coughing and somewhat disorientated; he can't take any more of this mad life! As Elliott tried to leap for the gun- he picked it up and pulled the trigger and: click! Click! Nothing happened! Harold smiled and walked towards him, "what's the matter out of bullets boy?" this time Elliott removed the safety switch and KA'BLooM!!! That was all it took! Elliott shot Harold; as Harold fell to the floor like an elephant- Elliott Jay looked at him and said, "NEVER OUT OF BULLETS BIG MAN, BUT YOU'RE NOW OUT OF TIME!" Elliott dropped his gun to the floor and rushed over to pick up his little helpless child- Harold was staring lifeless into the air, (he took his last breath). The feds were banging on the door, they rushed in! "What happened?" "We didn't even know how he got past us?"- The feds got on the phone, they were talking on their radios; it was a huge commotion, all you could hear was noise and radio frequencies* As Elliott was walking out of his room (it seemed like slow motion) he had his child in his arms, he went to go sit downstairs in his favorite chair) //

at the same time; more feds were walking by him- (upstairs) he is now having visions of his "beloved" beautiful girlfriend; Rainbow, as he sits down with his infant on his lap.

(Hearing the music in his head- Endless love)

THE END

Music by: kurtj c2009 and: -
www.myspace.com/kurtjxxx

http://www.amazon.com/The-Street-Team/dp/
B002PMHMCA

Would you like to see your manuscript become a book?

If you are interested in becoming a PublishAmerica author, please submit your manuscript for possible publication to us at:

mybook@publishamerica.com

You may also mail in your manuscript to:

**PublishAmerica
PO Box 151
Frederick, MD 21705**

www.publishamerica.com